Material
Things

Selina Rosen

Material Things
Selina Rosen
Second Edition Copyright © Selina Rosen, 2023

Published by Yard Dog Press at Kindle

Print Version ISBN 978-1-945941-39-9
Material Things
First Edition Copyright © Selina Rosen, 2004
Second Edition Copyright © Selina Rosen, 2023

Yard Dog Press
710 W. Redbud Lane
Alma, AR 72921-7247

http://www.yarddogpress.com

Edited by Sherri Dean
Copy Editor & Technical Editor Lynn Rosen
Cover art by Sherri Dean

Second Print Edition June 15, 2023
Printed in the United States of America
0 9 8 7 6 5 4 3 2

Table of Contents

Selina Rosen

Chapter One

"We have way more than our share of retards." That's what I thought as I passed the fifty-year-old guy with the bike helmet swerving and peddling like he was in slow motion. It's sort of funny the things that go through your head in the middle of a crisis. People like to think that your mind becomes consumed with the current or impending disaster, but it doesn't. It flops around thinking things like, "Where did I put my check book?" and, "Why are there so many retards in our county?"

Now I know what you're thinking - that I'm some sort of harsh bitch who doesn't give a shit about the whole politically correct thing - and that would make you right. The truth is I don't discriminate against the mentally challenged nor do I poke fun at the "special" people, I just believe in calling a spade a spade. Someone's *special* because they can obtain any sort of level of success in this crazy world of ours, not because they can barely drive a bike down the road at fifty-years-old, and what makes the term "mentally challenged" any better than "retarded"?

That's not the point. The point is that I was going through this huge family tragedy, and as I was driving to the hospital I just kept thinking the most trivial and mundane shit. I actually wanted to focus on my dad and what was going on with him because in our family everyone looks to me for the answers. I guess the real problem was that I didn't have any.

There's the real rub see, because we don't know what's best. Once someone's in the hospital undergoing medical treatment we're basically completely in the hands of the doctor and medical staff of the hospital. We're making choices that concern someone we care about, and we don't really have the knowledge we need to make informed decisions. One thing's for damned sure, the doctors aren't going to tell you shit—not unless you ask them direct questions, and even then they make it pretty damn obvious that they resent you asking.

Me… well I know just enough about medicine to know I don't know enough to make an informed decision about possible treatments. And I know for a fact that the hospitals—which are all owned by

1

money-grubbing, greedy corporations these days—want to make as much money as possible on each patient. If they have to jeopardize the health and mental well being of the patient in the quest of the almighty dollar, they will do so.

I have trust issues.

So… how do you choose, what should you sign, when do you demand answers, when do you sit idly by and let the hospital make all the decisions even when you think they're wrong? And of course the real problem is that my sister, my brother in-law, my brother, and my mother all have the ultimate faith in the doctors and hospitals. They have their heads firmly shoved up their asses and truly believe that no medical professional would ever endanger a patient's life for profit, much less lie about what was happening to them just to save the hospital and doctor a piss load of money in legal fees.

Oh how I wish the world were really the way they think it is.

But it's not.

The night before they performed abdominal surgery on my father to correct a section of bowel that was stuck up in a hernia in his stomach lining, he'd been in a lot of pain. But the surgery should have been fairly simple, and it should have been done immediately to stop any damage that might be being done to that strangled section of bowel. So, what did they do? They drugged him up with painkillers and did the surgery thirty-six hours later. The surgery went well, and fortunately his bowel hadn't taken any permanent damage. However, he had aspirated and sucked some gunk into his lungs, so he was going to have a ventilator breathing for him and would be in ICU for at least a week.

He hadn't been awake when I'd left after the surgery to go home and get some sleep. My mother and brother had stayed the night in the hospital ICU waiting room sleeping in chairs. I didn't feel like I was a shitty daughter because I didn't stay up there. My brother was just staying because my mother was—because he really believes she's this fragile bird, which she's not. I'll explain how I know this later—and my mother was only staying because she was afraid to leave, not because she could actually do anything.

I didn't know what I expected when I got to the hospital the next day. My father—possibly the oldest living, untreated, undiagnosed manic-depressive in the world—is a difficult person under the best of circumstances. He's a mixed bag of tricks, and you never knew what you'll get.

When I got to the hospital my brother had already gone to work, and my sister had started her vacation and had informed us that she'd be sleeping in. That's what Vicky does—takes care of herself first. Oh, she makes a good show of being more upset than either Ted or I, but the truth is that it's just that, a show. My sister got a lot less of our father's abuse than either me or my brother, yet she seems to harbor the most lasting resentment. If he died tomorrow I don't think she'd really care. She'd put on a big show, and mother would buy it, but my father's death wouldn't change her life much at all. Hell, she hardly even sees our parents anymore—even though she actually lives closer to them than I do. My brother and I on the other hand… Well we've even on occasion told each other that we'd be better off if the old man was dead because he just leaves a constant taint on our lives, but the truth is that… Well, Dad's like the little girl with the curl right in the middle of her forehead—when he's good, he's very good, and when he's bad… well he's horrid. But me and Ted, well he's also shaped our lives in so many positive ways. I mean yeah, we're a couple of the most screwed up, neurotic people you ever want to meet, but we'd just be ordinary, dull people without his input.

Hmm… Maybe that's why Vicky is so pissed off, because she's mostly just normal, so she got the nervous tick without the perks.

Anyway, when my dad goes we may not show it, but Ted and I will be devastated, because as much as we sometimes hate him, we also love him more than most anyone else in our lives.

Mom wanted to go see if Dad was awake yet, so we went back to his room. The hallway of an ICU is like a tunnel of weirdness. Even if you haven't been shoved full of twenty different kinds of drugs it feels like a different world.

When we got to his cubicle Dad was awake. Of course he couldn't talk because he had tubes rammed down his throat into his lungs. He was obviously in some sort of a panic, trying to tell us something that he couldn't, so the RN on his case suggested a pad and pencil.

Dad's wrists were strapped to the bed, and the first couple of lines he made looked like chicken scratch.

"Don't eat… Something I can't make it out," Mom said.

Mom's only five-six, so I look over her shoulder at the pad. "No… I think that's an I… I something."

Material Things

He flapped his arms around as much as the restraints would allow, obviously pissed off and even more panicked. He jerked at the strap and looked at me, so I freed his arm. The nurse immediately came in and started redoing the strap.

"Don't let him go, he'll pull out the breathing tube or his shunt." They had put a shunt in a main artery around his throat to hook the IV's up to because we all have such shitty veins.

"Sorry," I said. Dad looked defeated, but tried to write again. It's hard to explain to other people who don't know our family dynamics, but as children when Dad said "jump" we yelled back "how high and how far, sir!" Even as adults it's hard to just completely blow him off. Even when we do it still nags at us that we aren't doing what we're told. So when my dad's laying there like some human pincushion looking like the devil's at his feet and he's trying to write but he can't and he wants me to undo his arm… I do it.

Anyway he wrote something out and then Mom and I looked at it.

"Chalk?" I say.

"Choke," Mom says eye's wide. "Are you choking?"

He nods his head emphatically up and down.

"My dad's choking," I tell the nurse who's still milling around the room.

"A lot of patients on the ventilator think that, but let me check his airway." She winds up sucking a bunch of shit out of the tube and his mouth. "Is that better?" Dad nods his head yes, and I wonder why some nurses find it necessary to talk to old people like they would talk to a grade school child. Of course, personally, I don't talk to kids that way, either, and hearing it puts my teeth on edge especially when they are talking to my father—who's the meanest old son of a bitch who ever lived.

Calming down, my dad then writes almost too clearly. *Don't touch me.* And then—pointing at me—*Don't fuck with me.* We leave the ICU and go back to the waiting room. My sister Vicky shows up at 2:00 that afternoon and Dad wakes up and smiles at her.

I get *Don't Fuck with me*, Ted gets an order to go back to work, and Vicky gets a smile. It's more or less typical for our family. Vicky, who can barely stand Dad, can do nothing wrong. Ted and I, who bend over backwards for our dad, can do nothing right.

Dad seems to be doing all right, looking better, but Mother has decided that she's staying in the ICU waiting room again. Ted has to get some sleep or he can't work, and since he basically works for my dad it's important that Ted go to work. I write for a living, so none of them actually ever consider that I'm not on a permanent vacation. The end result is that I get very little sleep and I work at least part time for my father, but don't get paid since… "Donna doesn't need money."

Why doesn't Donna need money? The average American writer makes about seven thousand dollars a year. I make about two thousand under that, but I don't have any kids—my brother has two, my sister has three—and I'm not legally married. I'm queer, they all know it, and they know that I've been living with Amy for the last ten years, but somehow my relationship is only really ever important when they're considering that I don't need any money because, after all, Amy makes good money.

She has a decent job as a CPA, but she doesn't make *good* money. In fact, it's only the fact that I raise a huge garden and shop at railroad damage places that we can even make the ends meet.

But since Amy "supports" me—a fact which my father likes to rub in on a regular basis—it means I "don't need" money, and since I'm not in a "real" relationship with a house full of kids and don't have a "real" job, they expect me to drop everything anytime they need something and devote myself to them.

I don't think Amy gets as tired of this behavior as I do, but then it doesn't increase her workload at all or have her working when she should be sleeping.

Any way, it's decided that I will spend the night in the ICU waiting room with mother and forty other people—including ten Mexicans who've decided the ICU waiting room is a good place to play cards till 1:00 in the morning, and apparently assume that since we can't understand them we also can't hear them. Just before we lie down to sleep, Mom in her recliner—which she makes a point of telling me Vicky got for her, as if Vicky rode in on a white charger sword in hand and took on three black knights to win her the coveted chair—and me on the three-foot long torture couch of death, we go to check on Dad. I know at once that something isn't right. He's way too quiet. I go and find his nurse and talk to him. At this point he had the female nurse in the daytime and this guy at night. Two nurses, no more no less.

"We had to sedate him."

I wasn't too surprised. Like I said, Dad can be a handful on a good day. But there was something in his voice, and since my mother was busy standing by my dad's bedside as if that might be helpful, I ask., "Why did you have to sedate him?"

"He was giving us fits, pulling against his restraints, trying to get free."

This didn't surprise me either; still I could tell there was something he wasn't telling me. "Why was he so upset?"

"He's got the DTs."

For a minute that just didn't register. Not because my dad wasn't a big drinker, hell we hardly ever saw him that he didn't have a beer can in his hand, but he never drank hard liquor. I mean *never.*

"What's that?" I ask, because like I said it didn't register. I mean I know what DT's are.

"He's detoxing."

"Like a drunk in jail?" I ask because it's still not really registering.

"Yes," he said. Then he explained just what was happening to Dad.

For four days he hadn't poured any poison into his system and suddenly his liver was saying, "Hey no new poison! Good time to process this crap that's been building up." So it just starts processing and dumping all these chemicals it's been storing up. That's what causes the DT's, what makes people shake and get aggressive, angry. There's all this crap in their systems without the buzz that they're used to. Anyway it was further complicating Dad's recovery, which was just what we needed right then.

I thought about not telling my mom because she's been in denial about Dad's alcoholism just like she's been in denial about so many things. Hell, I'd been out and living with Amy for five years before Mom stopped being in denial about my homosexuality. When we got back to the ICU waiting room I knew I had to tell Mom because she needed to know what was going on. So I told her what the male nurse had told me, and … Well, she was mostly in denial.

We tried to sleep. I know it took me hours, but I finally drifted off. I thought I had slept quite awhile when a cell phone went off. I looked at the clock and it was 2:00 AM. I'd slept about ten minutes. I tried to get comfortable. Impossible, a five-foot ten-inch, forty-year-old woman can not get comfortable on a three-foot couch under the best of circumstances, but in the ICU waiting room it was impossible. These couches had wooden arms as high as the back and the seats were covered in vinyl. It's pretty obvious they don't really want people to stay there. I looked at the clock after twenty minutes of fidgeting, and then I looked over at my mother who was sawing logs and obviously sound asleep. She could sleep sitting straight up on broken rocks during a tornado. I realized there was no sense at all in me being at the hospital. I wrote a note telling my mother I'd be back in the morning, stuck it on her stomach, and went home.

Amy was sound asleep when I got home, but of course I fixed that when I crawled into bed with her making as much noise and moving the bed as much as possible.

"How's your dad?" she asked sleepily as I scooted up against her back.

"He's DT-ing, can you believe that shit? On top of everything else now he's DT-ing."

"What's that?" She asked.

"You know like drunks do when they dry out."

"Oh," she said, and then she was asleep. I really needed to talk, but of course she just went back to sleep. That's Amy. She's a good partner for the most part, very supportive of my writing—she thinks I'm going to be a big star someday and make lots of money. You'd think after ten years she would realize the folly of her ways, but no. She's also very supportive of the demands my family puts on me, but not so much that she'll actually go out of her way. If it's something she wants to do, she'll do it. If it doesn't cost her any sleep, or put her too far out then she's right there cheering me on, but the sad truth is that in the ten years we've been together anytime I've really needed her I've felt like I was mostly on my own.

She's a lot like my mother. She really wants to help, but she doesn't know how, and she doesn't really understand why you need so much help because she doesn't need it.

See… I'm manic-depressive, too. I've been diagnosed, but I won't do the medication. I just try to remind myself that *I'm* the one who's crazy. It works most of the time.

It's hard for people like my mom and Amy to understand what goes on in mine and my dad's heads. How the same thing that makes us so creative and passionate also makes us so miserable and difficult.

Amy and I used to have a much better relationship. She used to work really hard to try to make me happy, to try to make sure she didn't aggravate me or make things worse, but a few years ago all that stopped. I couldn't really tell you exactly when, and I don't know why. Maybe I was so needy I just burned her out. Maybe she just got tired of never really being able to fix things. Whatever the case I had watched as a certain coldness and distance entered our relationship. She was still there and still supportive and we still shared our lives, hell we even still had a healthy sex life, but there was something gone that had been there before. I had killed some little spark she'd kindled for me, and not knowing how I had done it, I didn't know how to fix it.

So I lay there that awful night, so exhausted I could hardly breathe, unable to sleep because everything was a mess, and having somehow destroyed my relationship I was on my own to deal with all my problems.

Again.

And make no doubt; everything that was happening with my father was my problem. I was no doubt the most damaged of my father's kids, but it was always up to me to fix things when they broke, even when they couldn't actually be fixed. If I screwed up, the wrath of my father came down on my head. In fact, if either Ted or Vicky screwed up it somehow miraculously became my fault, even if I was six states away at a convention at the time. In fact, just my being gone was more often than not what he blamed everything on. If only I was home where I belonged instead of careening all over the country pretending to be a writer…

Now, see? I know what you're thinking. Why do I give a shit about what happens to this drunken, abusive bastard who obviously has no respect at all for me? Well duh, he's my dad. He's my dad, and a few years ago I realized that at least in part he is now and always has been harder on me than he is the other kids because he knows—though I tried to deny it for so many years—that I'm the one who's the most like him. He doesn't want me to be because he knows how hard it is to be him. He'll never admit that there is anything wrong with his head, but I know he knows there is, and he knows what Amy and Ted and mother don't know. He knows what it's like to have a brain that screws with you. He knows what it's like to wake up one morning and feel like you own the world and to wake up the next and feel like someone has just stolen your last cookie.

Selina Rosen

There were times in my life when you would have had a hell of a time convincing me that he ever in his life curbed his rage; God knows I was the brunt of that rage more times than I can count. But I know what rage is inside me, and I know that it's a constant effort to keep it inside. It's like a caged beast that wants out and you know that if you let it out you'll feel better, but you also know that you may not ever be able to get it back in that cage.

And here's the real kicker. You can't live with other people if you always give in to your mood swings because it isn't fair to them, and you just might kill someone.

My dad never killed any of us. He never broke any of our bones or put us in the hospital. Now I know to most of you that hardly sounds like that big a deal, but then you don't know what it's like to have his brain—and I do. I know what I'm capable of, what I have to fight, and I know sometimes that in spite of my best efforts my anger erupts on those around me, especially those I love most. When I was younger I used to just smack anyone who pissed me off. Then I would just explode the way I'd always seen my dad explode. Unfortunately, what I learned from my father's violent tirades was true in my own life—no one will listen to you, no one will even care that they've hurt, upset or used you - until you start throwing punches or screaming obscenities.

The most horrible truth about having a bad temper is that it works. And the worst thing for me about what's happened with Amy and I is that I don't know if it was my opening up and letting the demon out of my brain one too many times, or if it was because I quit throwing the fits. See I don't ever completely lose it any more. I want to, but I just don't because I know it's wrong.

Let me explain. About six years into mine and Amy's relationship I hit a real bad depressive period. It was the funk to end all funks, and I guess I was contemplating suicide every other minute. My career had stalled out for like the sixth time—believe it or not, making five thousand dollars a year puts my career at an all time high. That's why Dad's little jabs about my "career" and Amy supporting me sting so bad, because I know I'm a big fucking loser. Anyway, Amy asked me to go to the doctor. He, of course, decided I had clinical depression—without asking me even a handful of questions—and he wrote me out a prescription for antidepressants.

Now here's the thing. I almost immediately felt better and thought

Material Things

I was cured, but apparently everyone around me thought I'd just finally gone all the way round the bend.

See, we bi-polar people *like* the manic periods, even when we're raging ass holes *we* feel good, and that can be quite the deal for us.

I guess she ran out of options and Amy talked to a friend of hers that was a shrink. Gloria was shocked and yelled, "You can't give Donna antidepressants, she'll go nuts! When you give a manic-depressive antidepressants you throw them into a manic episode."

"But Donna's not manic-depressive," Amy assured her, at which point Gloria no doubt gave her that "You're an idiot" look that over-educated people are so good at, and said basically that I was a textbook case.

So that's how I was diagnosed. Gloria gave me a test—which I passed with flying colors—insuring my status in the not-quite-sane-zone of psychotherapy, and then took me off the antidepressants and tried to put me on Lithium.

No one understands why so many manic-depressives won't take Lithium, but it's a no brainer, really. Just talk to anyone who's been on it. Oh it's true you don't have the lows, but you also don't have the highs. You're still depressed, but don't have either the ambition or the energy to actually even think about killing yourself, and because of this people think you're normal? If that's normal I don't want any part of it.

So I handle my problem without medication, but just knowing what's wrong is a big help. I think about the way I feel—or try to—before I act on it. So I don't blow up any more, and the people in my life have stopped walking around me like they're on eggshells the way we always have my father.

But now my partner and I just sort of live together. The spark's gone, and I don't know why.

Chapter Two

I don't know what I hate more, doctors and their pompous *I know everything and you need to know nothing because how could it possibly help* attitude, or hospitals and their purposefully foreboding atmosphere.

The second day of Dad's ICU incarceration started with him still heavily sedated and a consultation with his surgeon—who not only denied knowledge of my dad's aspirating (which was more than a little puzzling since he was the one who'd told us about it in the first place) but also managed to look shocked at the suggestion. Then we talked to my dad's nurse, who carefully explained what they were doing about his DTs and about the chemical pneumonia he was suffering as a result of aspirating prior to surgery.

Then we had a consultation with the lung specialist who my brother would later say was as worthless as ball sweat, then shouted, "No wait! At least ball sweat keeps your pecker cool."

"We're afraid Mr. Kingsly may have some chronic lung disorder. His CO_2 levels are very high."

"The nurse said that could be from the DTs," I said.

"Your father is DT-ing?" He sounded incredulous, and at that point I was fighting that little demon in my brain because I really wanted to smack him upside the head. He obviously hadn't even looked at my father's chart.

"That's what we were told by his nurses," I said. He shot an angry look down the hall at the back of a nurse.

"Well, that could be contributing, but his lungs are filled with fluid and we're going to have to schedule a CAT scan for him to determine what's wrong with his lungs."

"I thought they knew what was wrong, that he'd aspirated on the operating table."

He shot another dirty look down the hall at the nurse. "I don't have any knowledge of that."

"Well that's what we were told," I said.

"Well I wish you could find me someone who saw it happen." He had an accusatory note to his voice.

I bit my tongue, took a deep breath and asked, "If he'd aspirated what would you do for that?"

"We'd stick a tube down his throat into his lungs and suck the clots and fluid out."

So three hours later they took Dad to have a fourteen hundred dollar catscan, and twenty-four hours after that they suctioned the chunks from his lungs and were still insisting that Dad hadn't aspirated.

Right after our consultation with the lung man, after the procedure, was when Ted made his observation about ball sweat

Dad was still completely knocked out, and my mother, both my siblings and I were sitting in the waiting room. My mother and sister were basically telling me to shut up—without using those exact words because they haven't forgotten that I can blow up just like Dad does and they don't want a scene in the hospital—they don't want to hear my conspiracy theories. No one's lying to us about Dad's condition.

"You heard what they said, Donna," Mom says in that same soothing tone she uses on my father when he's in full beast mode—if she's talking at all. "Dad had pneumonia when we brought him in here."

"And they didn't figure that out in the more than thirty-six hours before his surgery," I said incredulously.

Then Vicky starts talking to me like I'm a total idiot. Since I have blown farts with a higher IQ than she has, I'm immediately pissed off.

"Donna." Sigh for effect. "They weren't expecting that. He was having stomach surgery."

My brother is silent, and surprisingly this pisses me off more than anything else because I know just by looking at him that he agrees with me. He knows something isn't right. He remembers the doctor telling us that first night that Dad had aspirated, and like me can't think of any reason for them to be lying to us now if that's just one of those things that happen.

I ignore my brother's silence, turn to my sister and talk to her in the same condescending tone she is using on me. "Vicky." Sigh for effect. "They ran like fifty blood tests, took urine and salvia samples. Don't you think they would have found something if there was anything to find?"

"Don't you start with me," Vicky hisses. "You're the head case, remember? This isn't one of your books."

Before I can murder my sister in the ICU waiting room, Amy walks in. It's 2:00 in the afternoon, and Amy's supposed to be at work, so I know one of them called her. No doubt because they figured I was about to flip out. Amy's got that look on her face that's a mixture of relief because I'm obviously not doing anything yet and dread because she knows that I still could.

I take a deep breath and stand up. My sister cringes, and I'm taken to another time. A time when my dad was mad and he stood up. I was the one who cringed then, and he whipped me with a belt for ten minutes, screaming at me the entire time for flinching.

I wasn't going to hit my sister, but I wanted to.

I don't want to be like him, at least not *that* him. Vicky's a spoiled little yuppie shit. But she's also my baby sister and I love her, and even though her opinions are always self-serving she still has a right to them. My dad never allows anyone to voice an opinion that isn't his, and like I said, I don't want to be like him.

Amy looks at me and says in a soothing voice. "How's your dad?"

It shouldn't have been, but it was the wrong question. I just wanted to scream that the hospital was trying to kill him and my stupid assed family would rather let the fucking hospital steal all our money and kill our father than say anything that might upset the doctors.

My brain was on fire from all the shit I wasn't doing or saying, and they were all pissed off because of the little bit that was spilling out of my mouth, and this is why I forgive my father for all the atrocities of my youth. Because I know that of all the people in my life, he's the only one who understands this god-awful feeling.

I don't say anything, and then Amy says something that almost immediately calms me down. "Come on, baby, let's go."

She takes my hand and gently guides me out of the ICU waiting room. She never holds my hand in public. We live in the south, where a lesbian couple showing simple affection out in broad daylight… Well, that's a good way to get your ass kicked or lose your job.

Next time you're in or around a hospital, take a second to look around you. People are more polite to each other; you see more couples holding hands. Old up-tight looking people who probably haven't touched in years will hold hands as they walk through the parking lot back to their cars. People walking alone seem even more alone, and the looks on their faces almost always seem haunted.

Amy leads me out of the hospital. I don't know where she's taking me, and I don't care. In the car I realize that I'm crying; I don't know how long I have been. I look over at Amy and she's got a determined look on her face, just focusing on driving.

I still love her. I know she still loves me, but something's gone and I miss it. I wonder what it is again even as I wipe my face and try to calm down.

"You alright?" Amy asked carefully.

I just nod my head because I'm afraid to open my mouth. Afraid of what might come out. Amy didn't do anything to incur my wrath, but she's not helping, either, and when I get like that, just not helping is enough to make me say some pretty horrible things.

I feel like shit. I feel like shit and she doesn't. I hurt and I just want someone else to hurt as much as I do, but I know it's not right. In the past when I've let my anger flow I've said the most terrible things I can think of to say, the most hurtful things. All the while, in my head I'm telling myself to shut up, not to say it, but once I get started I just don't seem to be able to stop.

It's a totally helpless feeling.

No, I ain't no schizo bitch. The voice in my head is still me, it's just more logical than the me that's talking. See I know I'll be sorry later, but at the time it just feels so good to just let go. To give in to that base instinct.

You can't really be yourself, at least not when you're like me. You often feel completely disconnected from yourself and the world around you like you're just floating somewhere watching yourself, helpless to control the things that happen to you.

I don't answer Amy's question. At that moment I don't really believe that she cares whether I'm all right or not. She's like the rest of them, she doesn't really care how I feel, doesn't really care if she can help me or not, she just wants me to pretend to be normal. To shut up and be quiet and let the hospital get away with whatever little scam they're pulling, just as long as there isn't a scene.

I think people worry too much about making a scene. Face it, ninety percent of the people you run into in any given day you'll likely never see again, so why the fuck should you care what they think of you?

My partner and my family seem to care more about how everyone else feels than they do how I feel. I know Dad must feel the same way.

Of course the brutal discipline and the insanity I grew up in is at least in part to blame for the mess that's in my head. In which case why should I have been upset at all that someone was torturing the old son of a bitch?

But I was.

I just said, "Where you taking me, the ha, ha Hilton?"

She smiled; she has a great smile. I find myself feeling some better as I realize that her smile is genuine even if it's most probably just because she's glad that I don't seem to be ready to blow. I don't like to cry. If there's a choice between crying and throwing a screaming shit fit, I'll damn near always choose the latter.

"Just away from there. Where do you want to go?"

"Let's go get something to eat," I say. I'm a 180-pound, five-foot ten-inch woman, what can I say? I like to eat. I'd been mostly on a diet and going to the gym three times a week for the last six months, but since Dad had been in the hospital everything was going to hell in a hand basket anyway.

"Where do you want to eat?"

"Some place where they add extra carbs and fat."

Amy laughs and turns the car towards El Super Taco Burrito.

See, here's something the Atkins people don't want you to find out. Do you know why people eat fattening food stuffed full of carbohydrates when they're upset or depressed? Because it works, that's why. Eating carbs and fat combats depression. Of course being a huge fat ass depresses you, which makes you want to eat more… and this is just one of the many reasons that the world sucks so bad.

I ate six super tacos and a huge burrito and drank about a liter of coke. When I started to feel human I said, "I wasn't going to come unhinged, maybe get a little loud but not actually take anyone's head off. Except maybe Vicky's, and no great loss there after all. They say a roach can live a week without a head, and Vicky's at least as virulent as a cockroach. You could have stayed at work."

"I know that." No she didn't. "You know me. I'll take any excuse I can to get out of the office early. They don't need me; it's not like it's tax season or anything. So you want to tell me what's going on?"

"If you tell me who called you."

"Your mother," Amy said simply.

15

Material Things

I must have been all but red in the face and screaming for my mother to call Amy. Not because mother doesn't like Amy, she does, but because my mother just doesn't like to bother anyone, especially if they're at work. Hell, mother won't talk on the phone if she can get out of it.

I told Amy what was going on, and far from looking at me like I was from Mars, she said, "I remember the night you came home after his surgery. You told me that he'd aspirated and they had him on the ventilator." She looked thoughtful for a moment. "Yes, I know you did. How would you have come up with that if the surgeon didn't tell you?"

"Exactly," I said.

"Why is he lying about it?"

"That's what I want to know, but they all want to sit around with their thumbs up their asses and pretend like everything's normal. I mean I have no doubt that he was DT-ing. Hell, the mean old shithead's been drinking four to eight beers a day as long as I can remember, and he's sure as shit shaking like a leaf. Do I believe they had to sedate him because he was violent? Sure I do. But what's all this farting around with the ventilator, and why do they need to do a fourteen hundred dollar test to find out what we know they already knew? Something's not right."

Amy nodded, then said gently, "But honey... there's nothing you can do about it. At least not as long as your family isn't going to back you up. All you're doing is upsetting your mother and pissing Vicky off."

She was right. I hate it when she's right.

Chapter 3

Dad started getting better almost the minute they vacuumed out his lungs, and a day afterwards they removed the ventilator. That's when things really got crazy.

He woke up, could talk for the first time in days, and just started spouting the craziest bunch of crap you ever heard.

"I've been kidnapped by Mexicans and I'm being held in a liquor store. Everyone in here's drunk."

"Dad, you're in the hospital, you've been sick, you've had pneumonia," I said.

"Bullshit, that's all bullshit!" he yelled. "They're holding me for ransom, I tell you." He started laughing then. "Dumb fuckers don't know I don't have any money."

Then he was all serious again. "Ted, you'll get me out of here, won't you Ted?"

"You've been real sick, Dad. You can't leave here yet," Ted said. He looked like he just wanted to die. Like I said before, it's hard for us not to do what Dad tells us to do, and when he was doing it with such a pleading tone in his voice… Well, let's just say I was glad that at least for the moment he was focusing on Ted and not me. Of course it didn't last; it never does. Ted swallowed hard and added, "You have to stay here till you get well, Dad."

"I'm not sick, God dammit!" He started pulling on his restraints. "Why won't you help me, Ted?"

"Calm down, honey." Mom took his hand and he seemed to calm down. That's when a nurse we'd never seen before told us that we were upsetting him and that he was calmer when we weren't around. The very next day we'd be told by a completely different nurse that he might quit acting so crazy and realize where he was if we spent more time with him. Mom didn't know what to do, I was five seconds from being as crazy as Dad was, and Vicky decided she just needed a few days away. So she and her husband got in their car and went to Branson for a couple of days. They left their kids with her husband's folks, but only after asking me if I could watch them and getting annoyed with me when I said no, that I was busy with Mom and Dad in the hospital.

Vicky's so helpful.

As the nurse hustled us out, Dad screamed after our departing asses, "That's right, Donna, you play their little game. You just go on and when they kill me you can take all my money."

Dad was right the first time when he said he didn't have any money. I don't know why I always get singled out, why everything that ever happens is my fault, but it is. I know in part he was mad at me because he expected me to do something, and of course I wasn't because… Well, what the hell could I do? I didn't trust the hospital, I sure as hell didn't trust his doctors who I knew were lying to us, but what good would it do for me to raise hell when no one else in the family wanted me to?

A nurse went to try to calm Dad down and he yelled at her, "You know what would make my day, dumb ass?"

"No, Mr. Kingsley, what would make your day?"

"If I could kick your fat, ugly ass!" He started pulling against his restraints like crazy and trying to kick her. She had to call for an orderly. None of us even tried to help. I know they probably wondered why.

When we got back to the ICU waiting room and my mother got in her chair –quickly before anyone else could claim it—she said, and I swear she was completely sincere, "I think Dad's getting better."

"Mom," I said in disbelief, "he's crazier than a shit house rat."

"But his color is good," she defended.

People always do that when someone's sick. *Their color is good* or *their color is bad*, as if that's the most important indicator of health. Of course as it turned out that rosy color in his checks was caused from too much CO_2 in his blood stream.

"I don't care what color he is, Mom, he's talking crazy shit and trying to beat up his nurse," I said.

Mother looked a little confused. "He is acting awfully violent, and your father's never been a violent man."

Now you could have probably scraped the disbelief off both mine and Ted's face and sold it as cosmetics. Call it Essence Of Shock.

"Mother," I started, reminding myself to whisper, "he used to beat his kids. He used to get in fist fights with his brother."

"Oh," Mother seemed to think about that, "but he hasn't done anything like that in years.

"He screams at you constantly, he's threatened to shoot half the people in town, and less than a month ago he ran one of the venders out of ghost town with a shot gun."

"But he didn't really mean it," Mother said, and I momentarily find myself wishing that Amy would rationalize half the shit I do that my mother does for my father.

I start to yell something that started with, "Great shitting Jesus!" but then Ted sighed so loud that I could hear him. I think he's finally going to say something, but of course he doesn't. I think the last hair fell of his ass right then and there.

I took a great big cleansing breath and then let it out, and got up and went to the coffee machine. My mother could never admit the things my father had done, in part because she'd then have to admit that she'd let him do it. I guess the God's honest truth is that unless she had been wiling to leave him there really wasn't anything she could have done, and my mother could never have left my father even for her kids, because she was crazy in love with him. She still is.

I got the coffee and started back across the room with it. It would have been hard to carry three cups of coffee back across the waiting room if the cups had actually been full, but the machine only ever filled the cups about half way—guess you can't bitch for a quarter. I handed cups to my mom and Ted then sat back down just in time for the fifteen-year-old retarded girl who'd been shadowing us for the last three days to sit down across from me and say, "Is that hot chocolate?" a hopeful sound to her voice.

"No, it's coffee," I said. "Would you like a hot chocolate?"

She nodded her head eagerly. "Please."

I got her one and brought it back to her. "Thanks." She took it and went back across the room to play cards with some little kids who were there.

Ted laughed.

"What?" I asked, then took a sip of my coffee.

"How many cups of cocoa has that kid conned you out of?"

I just shrugged silently. I felt sorry for the kid, and Mom explained why to my brother.

"Her dad had a massive heart attack and her mother's with him all day. Poor little thing is up here all day by herself." She lowered her voice even more, "She's a little slow. I think she may be retarded."

Well duh. Like I said, we seem to have more than our fair share of retarded people in our county.

"She seems a little hyper, so maybe it's not helping that Donna keeps feeding her hot coco," Ted whispered back.

I just shrugged. The kid was scared. Who wouldn't be in that hellhole? But then to add insult to injury she wasn't nearly big enough for her age, and she was maybe like a ten year old mentally if you were kind. It sucks to always be the odd man out, and I should know I was a queer, creative kid growing up in a small southern town, with the weirdo hippie Dad who'd built the ghost town. Speaking of which.

"I'd better get back up the mountain," Ted said. He smiled then, "Ghost Town won't run itself you know."

My dad always said that. He could never go anywhere and stay for more than ten minutes because… "Ghost Town won't run itself you know." It was how he got out of staying at my sister's kid's birthday parties or any other family or social function that wasn't at his house in Ghost Town.

I watched Ted go with a feeling of dread. Dad was acting like a nut job, I didn't want to deal with it, and I didn't want to be in charge. I was sick to death of being in charge. I just wanted to kick back or go run Ghost Town and leave all this crap for someone else to handle. But Ted was never the idea man. Oh, don't get me wrong, Ted's creative as hell, but God love him I don't think Ted often has a logical thought. He's a hard worker, but while he's working his head is always in the clouds and when it comes to a real problem… Well, hell, when Ted was having trouble with his first wife he used to call me to ask what he should do, and when she ran off and left him with the two kids to raise I wound up having to move in with him to take care of them till Ted married his second wife, Shelia. I like Shelia. She's a good ole girl, she's good to my brother, and more importantly she's good to my nephews. She's intelligent, and that's a good thing, because I was tired of thinking for my little brother thirty years ago. My brother would do nothing but sit around and think about all the great things he was going to do someday if it wasn't for Shelia lighting a firecracker under his ass every once and awhile. His kids, Roy and Jack, are sixteen and fourteen now, and they still listen more to Shelia, or me than they do to Ted. I'll just let you take a guess who they call if they have a real problem.

I thought momentarily about having Shelia come do things at the hospital while I went to Ghost Town to help my brother but knew that wouldn't fly. It was like they reserved all the really shitty things for me. Like they really thought I was the only one capable of true problem solving.

It's completely insane when you think about it.

It's sort of like… well imagine you're in a boat and it's sinking and you run and get the craziest mother fucker on board and say, "Hey the boat's broken fix it." Now that doesn't make a hell of a lot of sense does it? Yet that's exactly what my family does to me. They'll all tell me and anyone else that will listen that I'm nuts out of my gourd, then pick up the phone and ask for my help any time they have the most trivial of problems. When there's a disaster they immediately lose any common sense they ever had, and there they are with something broken for me to fix. I don't think it ever dawns on any of them that I might not be quite the mental nightmare that I am if they ever even once tried to fix something without calling me.

Gloria says it's a codependent relationship that I have with my family. I'm still not sure what that means except that it has something to do with my total inability to tell any of them no.

Whenever I try to wheedle out of doing something for them… well they just make me feel like dog shit like my sister did when I wouldn't stop everything in the middle of bailing the water from the ship and watch her stinking, bratty-assed kids. Just once I'd like for them to wake up and realize "You know this isn't actually just Donna's problem or her problem at all, maybe we should… oh I don't know, postpone our trip to Branson and stay here and help shuttle Mom back and forth to the hospital. Or help with Ghost Town a little, something that isn't totally and completely self serving."

Gloria says it's my own fault because I make myself available to them. Of course Gloria also called me last week to ask if I could bring my truck and come help her move. I didn't hear her telling me to stop being such a door mat when Amy and I were carting box after box of crap up the stairs to her new apartment.

A few hours later when we went to see Dad he was still talking crazy shit, but now he was scared, and I'd never seen him scared before.

"My family I love my family." He was crying and tears were rolling down his face. "That's all a man has is his family." He started to sob then. "I'm so sorry that I'm always such an asshole."

I'm figuring that's as close to an actual apology as we're ever going to get from him, so I for one am taking it.

"You aren't an asshole, Ted," my mother whispers back, but I think she knows he really is.

"Yes I am. Yes I am." He takes my hand, but he's still restrained at the wrists and they've got him in this shirt-like thing that's actually tied to the bed. "Donna, I have to tell you, family, family's the most important thing."

"I know Dad," I say and I have to tell you I'm getting a little choked up now.

"Donna… you have to get me out of here. This is a terrible place, Donna. They do horrible things to people." He cried louder so that I had to strain to understand him. "They drop little babies on their heads to make them sick. They cut people up, hold them down and torture them. They raise the dead and the dead don't want to be raised. They just want to die. Ed wanted to die but they just kept bringing him back so that they could steal everything he'd worked his life away for. People say you shouldn't worry about the material things, but… when a man's gone what does he really leave behind? Not his kids, oh no not his kids, they're nothing like him. You aren't like me, Donna, you're you, and you aren't me. So it's just his stuff, what he built with his own two hands that's all he has, all he leaves behind. You can't take what you've worked for with you so you leave it behind. It's your legacy. It was his legacy. They're trying to take everything Ed ever worked for. Trying to take all he has away from his wife and his sons…"

"Dad," I said gently, "You are in the ICU, in the hospital, you've been very sick, but you're getting better now."

"What?" he asked, looking confused.

"You had surgery on your stomach, remember Dad?" I said.

"Yeah," his eyes looked clear for a moment, "my guts were falling out."

"That's right Dad, they fixed that, but you've had pneumonia and…" that was when I lost him.

"No, no I didn't. That's the crap they're telling you, but I didn't have pneumonia."

"Yes you do, honey," Mother said gently.

"Don't tell me, you don't know. You're just one of the ghosts. One of the ghosts haunting me trying to get me to do your bidding. Well I won't you hear me? I'm going to get out of here where you can't tell me what to do." He looked right at me then. "You, get a knife and cut these off," Dad ordered, tugging against the restraints again.

"I can't, Dad."

"Donna." He cried then, all traces of anger gone. "Don't play their game; don't be like them. Cut me loose and get me the fuck out of here."

"I can't, Dad."

"Then go away. You're going to let them take everything Ed's worked for."

The nurse had told us to talk only sense to him not to play along with his delusions, but I couldn't help myself.

"Dad… who the hell is Ed?"

"He's standing right there." He pointed to the corner as best he could. There was nothing there of course.

"Dad, there is no one there," I said.

"Of course not he's dead you dumb ass," Dad said, and then he started laughing for no reason whatsoever. Then he got real quiet and whispered. "They finally let him die, but not before they got everything he owned. You have to help him, Donna, you have to get his stuff back for his boys, for Ed's wife."

The nurse walked in then and stuck something in one of the IV tubes. She mouthed the word sedative, and I just nodded.

"Help Ed, Donna," Dad said, and then he was asleep.

I followed the nurse out of his room. "What the hell is wrong with my Dad? He's crazier than a shit house rat. I mean he's always a little off but he ain't a friggin' nut job."

"He's got something called ICU psychosis, it's a combination of being on the ventilator, all the different medications. and well quite frankly being in here. We have patients who've had half the medications your father's been on that get it."

"All right, this might seem like a stupid question, but if they know this place makes people nuts why don't they fix it so that it's more palatable?"

She just shrugged.

"What the hell are you giving him? Maybe all that crap you're giving him is making him nuts," I said. My mother stood at my shoulder then, no doubt in the *grab her if she goes nuts* position, but I didn't care.

"It's just a relaxer, Ms. Kingsley. You see how agitated he gets."

"What the hell is a relaxer? Is that anything like an antidepressant? Because I have to tell you that if it is, it's going to make him nuts because he's bi-polar."

"It doesn't say that in his chart," she said with that air of *I know more than you do* that always pisses me off anyway.

"I'm telling you that he is. I am, he's my dad, he's crazier than I am, so he's bi-polar."

She didn't say anything then just gave my mother a "please help me" look.

Mom put her hand on my shoulder. "Come on, Donna, let's go."

I nodded then gave the nurse my very best pleading look. "Could you just please check to see if the stuff they're giving my dad my be agitating instead of relaxing him?"

"Sure will," she said with a smile. She wasn't a bad little gal, just normal and more than a little intimidated by a huge, angry dyke.

Chapter Three

So this was how things had been running. Mom wouldn't leave the hospital except for the 6:30 PM to 8:00 PM that they closed the ICU and you couldn't get in at all—they actually do this twice a day, in the morning and in the evening - but I was damned if I was going to run her back and forth twice a day. I'm not *that* big a doormat.

I'd get up every morning, go by the bakery—which I'd never been to before and was apparently where the area hid all its yuppie scum—I'd get two plain bagels with smoked salmon cream cheese and go have breakfast with Mom in the ICU waiting room. She'd tell me what she knew about how Dad was doing, which was basically nothing because my mother never asked the nurses anything. We'd go in, see Dad, he'd say something crazy, then he'd be out again. I'd hang out with Mom for a couple of hours, during which time I'd quiz the nurses. Then I'd go up the mountain and help Ted with Ghost Town because he was trying to do everything that he normally did plus everything that both Mom and Dad did. Then I'd come back down, go back to the hospital, go in to check on Dad, pick up my mom, take her to mine and Amy's house—which was only twenty minutes away. Mom would take a bath and change into the clothes I'd brought her from the house. Then I'd make dinner, we'd eat, and I'd take her back to the hospital before 8:00. We'd check on Dad, I'd talk to the nurses, and we'd hang out in the ICU waiting room—sometimes with Ted—till 10:00 when they'd turn the lights off in most of the ICU waiting room. Mom would go to sleep, I'd go home where I'd find Amy already asleep, and I'd lay there most of the night just trying to figure out everything that was going to need to be done and whether they were actually killing my father on purpose or not and what if anything I could do if they were.

And I'd wonder why Amy couldn't get up for at least a few minutes and at least try to make me feel better.

When Dad had been sedated and basically slept off the DT's and then the ventilator for six days, I'd tried to get Mom to just go back home for the night. She wouldn't.

"But Mom," I sighed, "you can't talk to him. He's knocked out and

25

he's got a tube in his throat."

Mom had cried for the first time—not a lot. Then, when she'd contained herself she said, "He might wake up and want me, and if he wants me I have to be here. I don't want him to think that I don't care."

My mother won't leave the hospital on the off chance my father—who was in a near comma—might wake up and want to see her, and Amy won't stay up for ten extra minutes so that she can talk to me and try to help me figure out what I need to do the next day, just be there so that I have someone to talk to about all the shit that was going on in my head.

Amy can't handle it, she can't handle me, and she'd rather just remove herself from the problem and let me fix things on my own. Amy isn't as strong as my mother.

My brother and his boys and my sister and her husband all think Mom is this delicate, fragile thing, but she's not. She's quiet, and she's uncomplicated, but she's not stupid—and she certainly isn't fragile. Hell, she's lived with our father for forty-three years. If she weren't tough she'd never have made it.

Any rate about the third day of him being crazy as a son of a bitch we're all a little on edge. It's the evening—I couldn't tell you which day because they had all sort of run together for me at this point. I probably could have kept count if I had just counted my dad's nurses because he had two new ones every day—one for the night shift and one for the day shift.

Of course we're not supposed to all be in his room at the same time, but Dad had apparently told mother that he wanted to see all his kids, so nothing would do but that we all came into Dad's ICU room in spite of the big signs everywhere that said *No more than two family members per patient.*

Our family as a whole isn't real big on rules, not if we think they might be stupid, and between you and me we think most rules are stupid.

"Material things, it's all about the material things. Family. It's so important." He starts crying again. Vicky immediately starts to cry because… Well, that's what Vicky does best—she pretends to feel. "Family's important, but it's what you built with your own two hands, what you leave your family that's your legacy."

"We know Dad," Ted says.

"Ed," my dad obviously works at consoling himself, "Ed, he was a humble man. A good, hard-working man. He and his sons they built an empire all from scratch. Piece by piece. Ed worked his whole life with his boys to build everything they have and now those filthy evil bastards... I'm getting to the point Ed, give me a second to get to the point."

And that was the first time I got this feeling like someone was behind me, like icy fingers were running down my spine.

"They're going to take away everything Ed's ever worked for and put Ed's wife out in the street." He looked right at Vicky then. "Are you Ed's wife?"

"No, Dad, I'm Vicky," she cried.

"Damn, where's Ed's wife?" Dad asked.

"I'm right here, Ted," Mother said.

"Dammit, you're *my* wife. I know that. We have to tell Ed's wife, his sons, what the bastards have done." He looked at me, as if I were his last hope, "Donna?"

"Yeah, Dad?"

"Listen to me. You have to make sure these bastards don't get Ed's place. He's going to haunt me till the day I die if you don't stop them. You stop them, Donna."

"I will, Dad," I said.

"These are some evil bastards. Evil and they do evil things, you have to stop them."

"I will, Dad."

"Good. You're a good girl. I'm tired now."

He went to sleep. Feeling like we'd been whipped, we all went back to the ICU waiting room. Surprisingly, or maybe not, Vicky was the first one to talk.

"Donna, they told us not to agree with him when he's delusional."

"Shut the fuck up, Vicky!" I know what you're thinking—that I said it. But I didn't, it was my brother Ted making a grab to stick the hair back on his ass. "You've been gone for two days off having a vacation while we, especially Mom and Donna, have been dealing with Dad. Sometimes telling him the truth calms him down and sometimes going along with him calms him down, and we've learned to just play it by ear."

"I had to get away; I couldn't take it anymore." Vicky started crying again, and Mother patted her on the back. Mother's always been way too gullible when it comes to my sister.

I guess Ted had just finally had enough because he said, "Oh quit with the water works. We all know what's wrong with you. You thought Dad was going to give us some big touching moment and you could cry and act touched, but instead he just spouted a bunch of crazy shit at us. Well, welcome to our world, baby sister, we've been dealing with this shit for days."

"Screw you, Ted," Vicky screamed back.

I felt really good about what was unfolding in front of me. People were making a scene, and it wasn't me. It was a very enjoyable moment for me to just kick back and watch my siblings make a scene in public for a change.

"Now kids that's enough," Mother said in a whisper, looking around at all the people in the room who were gawking at her two "normal" children. Unfortunately they both got very quiet. "You're all just upset because you're worried about your father. He wasn't talking that crazy. I mean he is, but think about it. We know he's always been fascinated by ghosts. Hell, he built Ghost Town and Ted and Donna helped him build it and you know he always calls you his boys," A fact that I loved. "You know he's never trusted doctors. He's always been worried that he'd get sick and have to come here. That's why he waited as long as he did to get any help. Don't you see, kids? He's Ed. He's worked most of his life to create Ghost Town, and now he's afraid the medical bills are going to eat it up."

"Maybe they will, Mom," Ted said, and I could tell this wasn't the first time he'd thought about it. Hell, Ghost town was his livelihood, too. His home was also there. Dad had Medicare but anymore that won't cover everything.

"Don't worry, Ted, Dad doesn't know it but about three years ago I got supplemental insurance. We're completely covered now."

Now you might be asking why my mother would have to sneak around to get supplemental insurance and then hide the fact from my dad. You see Dad voted for the current administration—kind of shows you how I rate in his life when you realize that he has an openly gay child and he votes for a homophobic prick—and he truly believes that they haven't done any of the evil things that they have done. The war is necessary; the economy was ruined by the last administration, which he no doubt believes is also to blame for making policy that basically allows the medical community to get as much money out of us as they are capable of getting while the quality of care evaporates before our eyes. Further, the current administration is right—a person shouldn't be able to file for medical bankruptcy. These are the facts the way he sees it, and as I told you—in his mind—no one else has a right to their opposing opinion. Disagree with him and he'll scream in your face till you shut up.

The fact that the current administration is fully responsible for an economic climate that has all but ruined a business he has worked on his whole life doesn't seem to quite compute.

Ghost Town had been doing a booming business, all the stores were filled with vendors and it looked like it was going to turn into the gold mine that it was supposed to be built around. The Bush administration had almost killed my father's dream just like it had so many other people's, but he was still right behind him pushing. He blamed Clinton and the Democrats as the tourist trade started to dry up and one by one the venders started to leave. It didn't matter that "his" president was in office at the time. Slowly we're getting some vendors back, but it isn't because they've turned a corner, it's because they can't find jobs. The group we have in the shops now aren't as talented or as ambitious as the people we all grew up with. These people are hard up and they're looking for something they think will get them rich quick. Half the stores are no longer filled with beautiful arts and crafts, hand crafted by people right there at Ghost Town. No, half the shops are filled with cheap-assed Korean crap. The shops change venders so often now it's hard for me to keep up with them.

Mother wasn't quite as blind as Dad was to the facts, and she'd protected him, but if he ever knew he'd be madder than three sticks of dynamite up a black cat's ass. No one was likely to tell him, though, and since Mother took care of the bills, he'd most likely never find out.

If it wasn't for the fact that he'd worked so hard for everything he had, and if my brother, my mother and I hadn't worked just as hard for it, I'd say he deserved to have his business all but fold up and his medical bills sky rocket because he'd voted for the son of a bitch.

One of my publishers once told me, "Now, now Donna everyone who votes for Bush isn't stupid, some of them are evil." Still don't really know which category Dad fits into. He got caught up in the whole

Material Things

"Evil Democrats are trying to make America a Communist country" thing back in the 60's and 70's, and I don't think he's ever going to be able to let it go. It doesn't matter that the Republicans have now taken away all the rights that he was sure that the Communists/communists were going to take away from us, or that the corporations and religious right—both of which he hates—have taken over the Republican party. He watches Fox News exclusively and believes all the utter bullshit that Rush Limbaugh and other idiots like him say. He's just like all the ignorant bastards who sit around and bash liberals while the conservatives turn our country into a smoldering pile of dog crap. The difference is I know he's not stupid, he's just hard headed, and I think it's impossible for him to admit he's wrong, so... Well he isn't stupid, so he must be evil.

Problem solved.

Chapter Four

I bought Mom's "fable" explanation, and feeling really good about not being the kid to show my ass—at least on that day—I decided to let my sister and brother keep Mom company, and go home and spend some time with Amy. Of course when I got home a good hour earlier than I had been getting home Amy was still in bed fast asleep. I half think she saw my dad's hospitalization as sort of a mini-vacation.

I made a piss load of noise on purpose and she finally woke up. She stretched and looked at the clock. "You're home early."

"And yet you're still in bed asleep," I said with a tinge of anger in my voice.

"I was tired. I went to bed. Is that a crime?" she said in that long-suffering tone of voice I no longer find cute.

"Not if you're a second grader," I hissed out. I stomped into the bathroom to get a shower.

Now here's the thing. I'm the one with the defective brain, I'm the one everyone delights in telling that I'm somehow deficient, yet here's the cold hard facts. If I knew she was having a bad day, I wouldn't go to bed and go to sleep until she'd come home and had a chance to download. If I *did* go to sleep because I just couldn't stay awake any longer and she woke me up, I'd ask her how her day was. And if I could tell that she was pissed off, I'd make damn sure I was wide awake and ready to—at the very least—defend myself when she came back to bed.

It took me ten minutes tops to shower and when I walked back into the bedroom she was sound asleep again.

I fought the urge to wake her up and fight with her. Tell her just exactly how I felt about her non-existent partnering skills. It was one thing that most of the time she was just sort of there, and quite another thing when she wasn't there at all, and a hundred other really hurtful things that wouldn't do a damn thing to make her change and that I'd only wish I hadn't said even while I was actually saying them.

I just turned off the light, lay down, and tried to go to sleep. Of course, I couldn't sleep because I really just wanted to fight with my old lady. To try to get over my mad I tried to think about what my father

31

said and started wondering why he had always been so fascinated by ghosts. I remembered that cold feeling at my back, and I wondered if there might be any truth in what my dad was saying.

Then I remembered that since the surgery Dad spent most of the time he was awake trying to get people to look at his penis and tell him what was wrong with it. No matter who it was or how many times it was explained to him that he was catheterized, it just didn't soak in.

The next morning my mother wasn't in her chair, so I left the bagels there for her and I went to check on Dad. I ran into Mom in the hall.

"I was in the bathroom," she explained.

"I left breakfast in your chair. I think I'm going to go check on Dad."

Mom frowned. "If it's all right with you, I'm not going to go with you… Donna, he's in quite a mood this morning." I realized in that moment that even Mom was starting to have her doubts about Dad's treatment and recovery, and I think that unnerved me more than anything to that point.

"That's all right, Mom. If he's acting too nuts I won't stay."

As soon as I walked in Dad's room he pointed at a nurse standing in the hall—well, as best he could with his arm tied to the bed—and said, "That's her. That's the one. If she had a black dress and blond hair she'd be the perfect villain."

Dad started out as an artist, but he couldn't make a living so he started painting signs and made enough money to raise three kids and build Ghost Town. Now he painted pictures and ran the town to make his money. He should have been happy, but he still wasn't. He couldn't be, just like I couldn't be. Our brains just flat weren't built for contentment. Where am I going with this? Well, I got a little off track, but the point is that Dad's a painter, an artist, so color is important to him. That's why he wanted this nurse to have a costume change. Her color was all wrong to be wicked.

"She's a bad one, Donna, a bad one." The nurse taking care of Dad's IV lines at the time looked at me and smiled a reassuring smile. They kept telling us that he was going to get better at any moment. What I didn't seem to be able to make them understand was that he was difficult on good days, and he most probably was going to be a total asshole when he got out of here. He'd believe that he'd been tortured in here and that we'd allowed it to happen, and he'd make our lives a living, tormentuous hell.

I looked back at the nurse Dad was talking about. She was just staring in at us, and I wondered what her problem was. Lots of the people in ICU were as screwy as Dad, if not worse; he wasn't even the only one trying to hit his nurses. Hell, two days before a patient had actually succeeded in decking one of the nurses.

"It's in her locker, Donna. That's where Ed's Saint Christopher is. It's in her locker."

Now that just blew Mother's little fable theory to pieces because Dad was not now, nor had he ever been, religious. He was a devote agnostic who thought people who wore their religion around their necks were morons.

And yet he's a Republican. Like I said it just doesn't make sense.

"Dad… you don't have a Saint Christopher's medal."

"Christ! I know that, Donna. I told you it's Ed's. It was silver and she took it. She's a bad one, a bad one I tell you. Tell her Ed, tell Donna."

And I swear I felt like someone was at my back so much this time that I actually turned around.

"Check it out, Donna," he said.

"I will." I said. The nurse gave me a dirty look as she left. She was obviously of the school of *don't play into his psychosis*. "I've got to go, Dad." I looked around to make sure no one was around. "Dad, you've got to quit talking this crazy shit or you're never going to get out of here."

"I know." He started to cry. "They're not going to let me out of here if I don't shut up because they don't want anyone to know what they're doing. You've got to stop them, Donna. You've got to get me out of here."

"All right, Dad, I'll see what I can do, but you work on not being such a nut job."

He nodded and I left. I don't think he really understood me, but maybe he did. As I was leaving the ICU a young man was getting loud.

"My mother gave it to him in here," he said in an accusatory tone.

"Sir, we don't allow the patients to have any jewelry on this floor."

"I know all that. I'm telling you that my mother gave it to him anyway. That she put it on him. She wants to bury it with him."

"We don't have it, sir." It was *her*, the nurse Dad thought would make a great villain if only she was the right color.

"How do you know if you haven't even looked? It probably fell on the floor or something. Please."

"I'll tell the staff, and if anyone sees it..."

"They're burying my father tomorrow. I need it today. You people have taken everything my father's ever worked for. Surely to God you can take a few minutes to do this one small thing..."

"I'm sorry, you can see how busy we are."

"Could you please just check the room he was in? That's all I'm asking, just check his room."

"What was your father's name?" she asked, but I got the impression she already knew.

"Ed Cocks." I stopped in my tracks then and pretended to be waiting to talk to my dad's nurse. You know standing, looking to where she was working, checking my watch, looking back at the curtain where my dad slept.

I'm nothing if not stealthy.

"And what's the item again, sir?" I knew from the curt tone of her voice that she already knew that, too.

"A silver Saint Christopher's medal."

By this time I was all but shitting myself I was so weirded out. Before the nurse went off to pretend to look for it I caught her name off her nametag, Vera Terms. I kicked my better judgment right in the ass and walked up to Ed's son.

"I don't think she's going to find it," I said.

"Why not?" He was still angry. "How far could it have gone?"

"I don't think she's going to find it, because... Well, I think she took it. Could you come with me?" He looked at me like I was mad. "Please, what could it really hurt? I mean, what am I going to do, mug you right here in the hospital? It will only take a minute of your time."

He nodded and followed me. "Now my dad's been mostly completely out of his gourd for several days, but I think... Well I think if he's in the right mood... Well that you're going to be as freaked out as I am."

We walked into Dad's room and he was still awake. "Fucking Mexicans, you let me out of this liquor store," Dad yelled. There was of course no one in his room but us. I looked at Ed's son, smiled and shrugged.

"Hey Dad." I got closer to him and said in a lower voice, "I brought Ed's son."

Clarity seemed to wash over Dad's face as he looked at the young man.

"I knew you'd come through, Donna, you always do." I knew he was still crazy out of his shitting mind because he never would have said anything like that if he wasn't, mostly I get dumbass and fuck up. Dad looked at the man. "Listen, Jerry." The guy went white as a sheet, so I figured right off that Dad got his name right. "You can't just let them take everything your father worked for."

"How can I stop them?" Jerry asked in a trembling voice.

"They kept bringing him back. They kept bringing him back to get all his money. The proof is in the Saint Christopher, that's why she took it. She took it, you know which one, Donna." I nodded and then Dad said, "Donna?"

"Yeah, Dad?"

"You know what would be good?"

"No, what, Dad?"

"A big ole glass of Vodka."

I sighed and rolled my eyes. "Dad, you don't even drink Vodka."

"Sure I do. I love Vodka. Surely they have some Vodka in this liquor store."

"Dad, you're in the hospital. They don't have anything for you to drink but that crap." I motioned towards the multitude of IV bottles all plugged into that shunt.

Dad looked at them contemplatively then he looked back at me. "Do they have any Tequila?"

Dad didn't drink Tequila either, just a shit pot load of beer.

Then Dad looked at Jerry. "You a doctor?"

"No, Dad, he's Ed's son, Jerry."

Dad nodded and looked at Jerry. "Could you take a look and see what's wrong with my peter? They've done something to it."

I explained to Dad again about his catheter—for all the good it did—then said good-bye to Dad, and followed Jerry out of the room.

"What the hell is going on?" Jerry asked me. The nurse Dad hated, Vera Terms, walked up to us then.

Material Things

"I'm sorry, we couldn't find it."

Jerry started to protest and I grabbed his arm. "Come on, dear, there is nothing we can do about it now."

The nurse gave me an odd look, no doubt because I'm one of those dykes that just never could make a very believable straight person, and because she knew I belonged with Dad. I didn't care, I just wanted to get out of there and go someplace where we could talk. I asked Jerry to meet me in the cafeteria and went to tell my mother that I had to leave for a bit just so she wouldn't worry.

When I sat down at the table across from Jerry he didn't beat around the bush, "What the hell is going on?" he asked.

"You ever hear of Ghost Town?"

"That little village about twenty miles north of here?"

"Yeah. Well, my dad built that. We own it. I always… Well we always thought it was just something he'd created because he thought it was neat and it would make money, but now I'm thinking… Dad was in a car wreck when he was a young man; he was in a coma for days. I think maybe all the dope and the trauma made him see ghosts then and that's why he was so obsessed with them. I know it sounds crazy, but… Well, your dad died here didn't he?" Jerry nodded his head. "Then if there is such a thing as ghosts, he might be here, and I think… Well, I think my father is talking to your father. I realize that my father is crazier than old cooter's goat right now, but maybe that's why he can talk to the dead, maybe that's what this ICU psychosis really is, the drugs screwing with the brain and making the sick capable of communicating with the dead. Dad knew your dad's name, knew your name, and knew that your dad's medal was missing."

Jerry wasn't terribly hard to convince. "And he knew Mom's going to have to sell the Berry farm to pay the hospital bills."

"He said that nurse had it in her locker," I said.

"What did he mean they kept bringing him back? Dad had a DNR. He'd been on liver dialysis for a year; he had heart trouble and had destroyed his bladder so that he had to wear a catheter tube all the time. He didn't want to live, he just wanted to die with an ounce of dignity, but he just kept holding on. It was like his body was against him, even when it came to letting him die in peace instead of pieces."

It all clicked together then. What had happened to my dad, what they were doing in the ICU in that one and a half hours they closed it

36

in the morning and in the evening. I took in a deep breath, then let it out and said in a hushed whisper, "They're resuscitating the DNR's. They are purposely leaving patients sick without treating them for two or three days, and running unnecessary tests to make more money. That's why the Saint Christopher is what we need. If they resuscitated him when he was wearing it, well it was silver, right?"

"A good conductor. It would have left a burn on Dad's body," Jerry finished. "We've got to get that medal."

"I'll get the medal. You get to the funeral home and see if your father has a burn mark the size and shape of his medal on his body. If he does, call the police and get them back here."

He nodded, gave me his cell phone number, and we went our separate ways.

I made a B-line for the ICU nurses' lounge. There were two nurses in there who I'd seen on the floor. I decided it was more important to get the item out of Vera Term's locker than it was not to be seen doing it. She might have figured out we were on to her, might be even now coming to get the medal. Might have already moved it. I saw a box of latex gloves sitting on a table and pulled them on. The nurses just looked at me suspiciously, so I said, "Do you know who I am?"

"You're Mr. Kingsly's daughter."

I nodded. "I'm also an FBI agent."

"You're a writer. I have a couple of your books," the nurse named Betty said.

I was momentarily taken aback. I'd never run into anyone anywhere but a convention who'd read one of my books. "Really, which ones?"

"*Forever Monday*, and *Always Tuesday*," she said, then got that excited fan girl look on her face. "When is the third book coming out?"

"I don't really know when they're going to release it. I've turned it in, though." That was what I'd been told to say. I didn't want to tell her that sales on the second book had been so abysmal that there was a good chance the publisher wouldn't be releasing the third book at all. Have I mentioned how much my whole life just really sucks? "I could bring you a copy of the manuscript if you'd like."

"That would be great."

The nurse named Jean—who wasn't a rabid fan girl—reminded me of what I was supposed to be doing when she looked at my gloved hands and asked, "What are you doing in here?"

That's when I remembered that all the nurses on the floor's body language changed whenever Vera Terms was around. They didn't like her. And when people don't like someone they are more than willing to help you get them in trouble.

"I think that nurse, Vera Terms," they instantly made faces like someone had farted, so I knew I was on the right track, "I think she and some of the doctors are resuscitating people with DNRs."

"I told you, didn't I tell you?" Betty said to Jean.

"That's just crazy," Jean said.

"Really?" I asked. "What does it cost to keep a patient in the ICU on life support?"

"A fortune," Betty said.

"I was sure Mr. Cocks had a DNR, but they brought him back. When I said something to Dr. Green he insinuated I just wanted to lessen my workload," Jean said.

"Dr. Green is my dad's doctor, too. They sent Dad for a CAT scan to see what was wrong with his lungs after we'd already been told that he'd aspirated on the operating table."

This seemed to convince Jean completely. "What are you looking for?"

"Mr. Cock's wife had snuck his Saint Christopher's medal on him without the staff knowing. I know my dad's crazier than a shit house rat, but he told Mr. Cock's son that he saw nurse Terms take it. I just want to check her locker."

"It's this one," Betty said getting up and walking over to it. She kicked the bottom of it, pulled up on the latch, and it opened. I must have looked some surprised because she smiled and said—without missing a beat, "They're only lockers in the loosest sense of the word."

I quickly rifled through the contents of the locker. I was about to think I might as well just walk down the hall and turn myself into the psych ward when I found the medal in the pocket of one of nurse Term's smocks. I turned back to the two nurses who looked delighted and impressed. Having good-looking women looking at me like I'm just the cleverest thing they've ever seen is never bad for me.

Just then Nurse Terms walked in. She looked about three seconds from shitting all over herself when she saw me and what I had in my hand.

She turned as if to run, but nurse Betty stepped into the way. Terms just sort of looked defeated and slumped into a chai,r which was sort of a big disappointment for me because I really would have liked to sling her against the wall a couple of times just to impress my new groupies. As it was I just stepped close to her and looked down at her menacingly. "Looking for this?" I asked.

"Where did you find it?" Oh she was a cool one, this Vera Terms.

"In the pocket of your uniform in your locker," I said feeling very Mike Hammerish.

"And we were witnesses," Betty said excitedly.

"Anyone can get in those lockers," Vera said.

"True, but not everyone can resuscitate a body," I said. "Not everyone's finger prints are going to be on this medal."

I called Jerry on the cell phone and found that he had already called the police. They'd looked at the body and called in the county coroner to perform an autopsy.

They were already on their way to the hospital.

Material Things

Chapter Five

As luck would have it, the officer who'd answered Jerry's call had a grandparent who'd died a couple of months earlier in that hospital after a long stay in ICU. She'd also had a DNR, and he'd felt like she'd lived much longer than she should have.

Now I know that sounds like an odd thing to say, but it's true. None of us want to go like that—in pain, out of our heads, hooked up to machines, spending every dime we've made, leaving our loved ones with debt instead of the things we'd worked so hard to buy in our lifetime. When it's time to go, I just want to go, and so does everyone else. But the damn doctors and hospitals want the money, so they'll lie and tell a patient that with liver dialysis they can still have some quality of life. They'll tell you they can't tell if you have cancer or not unless you have a fourteen hundred dollar test, and you're completely and totally at their mercy. Here's the thing, they don't have any—mercy that is— at least these blood-sucking leeches didn't.

See it's all owned by the corporations now, and the same corporation that sells the supplies runs the hospital and makes the drugs, so they can jack the price of something up and tell you they have to charge that much because they have to pay so much, but it all goes right in the same pocket.

When the police got there they took the medal, put it in a baggy and started questioning the staff, and the real nightmare in terms of human suffering started to unfold. That very night three doctors and two nurses were arrested. And who was the person who gave the police the most information? Why it was my dad's first nurse, the one who had told us all about his aspiration and then we'd never seen again. It turned out that they'd been moving the nursing staff constantly so that they wouldn't know what was going on. You see Nurse Terms was the head nurse, and it was easy for her to work the schedules so that the nurses moved so much they didn't have a chance to catch on.

Sylvia—the nurse who had all the information—had been suspicious. She'd asked way too many questions, and so after the thing with Dad they'd moved her completely out of the ICU so she couldn't tell people's families what was going on.

By the time the investigation ended three months later, three hospital board members, five doctors, and four nurses had all been indicted. I think it goes deeper than that, though, I think it goes right up to the top of the little corporate heads, but in this brave new country of ours it's almost impossible to touch the super rich. No one really cares what I think anyway. After I'd given my testimony—Jerry and I both left out the part about Dad telling us what Jerry's dead father was telling him—I was more or less just dead weight, and the DA's office got tired of me hanging around trying to get them to listen to my conspiracy theories. They basically thanked me for what I'd done, patted me on my head, and asked me—in so many words—not to come back any more.

Once they took Dad off the meds he shouldn't have been on in the first place, and he had doctors who weren't criminals, he got better fast and we took him home. He's actually more appreciative of us these days. Even says nice things to us right to our face. Of course, between me and you, I think it helps that ever since he got out of the hospital beer tastes like piss to him. He's quit drinking. I don't know whether his new doctor told him he had to or not, I'm just glad he quit. Oh, don't get me wrong, Dad's still difficult, and he's still voting Republican, but at least he occasionally has something nice to say to us.

He says he doesn't remember anything about his ICU incarceration, and he sure as hell doesn't remember seeing any ghosts much less talking to them. I think he's full of shit. When I tried to get him to talk about it he just flat wouldn't admit to remembering any part of what he'd said or done.

Amy thinks I'm crazy. She doesn't believe in such things as spooks and stuff. I try to remind her that I didn't either until ghosts helped track down some seriously evil bastards, and she just says I'm so smart that I took the little things that Dad had accidentally heard and was butchering and put it all together till I figured out what was really going on.

In fact, Mom seems to be the only one who believes that Dad was talking to the ghost of Ed Cocks. My sister and brother, even Ed's son, Jerry, now seem to think that Dad just picked up pieces of conversations and figured it all out.

At least Amy gives me the credit.

I know what I felt, and I believe Dad was talking to a dead guy in the ICU. I ain't buying he figured anything out catching a little snip of conversation here and some there. First off you just can't hear that well in the ICU, and he doesn't hear that well anyway. Second off, my dad was intermittently insisting that they had done something awful to his pecker and that he was being held captive in a liquor store... Hey, maybe that's why he quit drinking. Maybe he's developed a fear of liquor stores. Have to ask Mom what she thinks.

Anyway, the way I see it if there are ghosts then what better place to find them than the friggin' hospital? After all, the way they work things these days that's where most everyone dies. It just makes sense to me that if there are ghosts the hospitals are full of them, and it also makes sense that the very sick would see them. After all, if you think about it, people in ICU are somewhere between here and there. They're only really half alive in there. Machines are breathing for them, feeding them, draining their bladders, and monitoring their vitals.

A couple of nights ago I remembered what I overheard one of the nurses saying to another. He said, "He looked up at me and he said, 'It's not an option,' and I said, 'What's not an option, sir?' and he said, 'Death it isn't an option. We all think that it is, but it's not.' I don't know why that shook me up so bad, but it did. I guess because he's right. I guess we all do think that death is somehow an option."

Well, maybe death isn't an option, but maybe, just maybe, the dead can hang around awhile after they die, especially if they have unfinished business. Like say some greedy corporation-owned hospital kept torturing them, keeping them alive as long as possible, so that they could take everything they worked for.

I believe in ghosts now. So does Mom, and while he won't admit it I know Dad knows they exist, too. I think, in fact, that he knows better than anyone.

I'm still writing for all the good it does. Amy's still thinking I'll strike gold at any minute. My brother still can't put two rational thoughts together without help, and my sister is still a flaming self-centered bitch. Life goes on.

I keep thinking—maybe obsessing's closer to the truth—about how good it felt to catch those guys and put an end to their reign of terror. It made me feel really good about myself, like I was actually making a difference. I have to tell you the truth, between being a writer and being a head case, that just doesn't happen much.

I'd like to end this by telling you that I figured out what was wrong between me and Amy and I fixed it—Wouldn't that be a great ending?—but the truth is that I figured out what's wrong and there is no fixing it, because there isn't really anything wrong.

It's just familiarity, that's all. It might not always breed contempt, but it certainly does dull things up. Ten years of putting up with each other's PMS and other idiosyncrasies, smelling each others farts, talking to each other when you're on the can, nursing each other through various illnesses where green phlegm is being hocked up and puking pink medicine occurs, well it sort of kills the romance.

Passion's a fleeting thing. It's there every once in awhile, but it's never what it was in the beginning. After a few years a relationship gets stale like old bread, but as long as there isn't any mold growing on it you keep it. Hell, sometimes if there's just a little mold you scrape it off and keep it any way. Same with a relationship. As long as it isn't really bad… Well you can live with bland.

I still love her, and she still loves me, and maybe after ten years that's a whole lot.

Part of the problem is that I have nothing else. Maybe if I had something to do, something exciting and meaningful, then I wouldn't be so needy, I wouldn't expect my relationship to fill all the gaps in my more or less meaningless life. My writing was supposed to do that, but it just doesn't any more because I know it's a huge deadend even if Amy doesn't.

I think that's why I'm obsessing about the whole hospital fiasco. I did something with meaning. I succeeded at something. People—at least for awhile—were treating me like I was something special. No, I didn't save any lives, but I saved people from being tortured. I saved families from bankruptcy.

Maybe that's what I need to do, give up writing and become a private detective. Do something exciting that gives my life meaning.

Outside my window I see the retarded guy ride past on his bike and I remember what Dad said about them purposely dropping babies on their heads.

About the Author, Selina Rosen

I started writing at twelve as an escape. The situations I have lived through are the stuff of which my fiction is born. My relationships with the many and varied people I have come into contact with over the years is a catalogue of characters from which I pull.

I am Jewish but consider myself spiritual not religious. I have studied every form of spirituality and try to live a spiritual life. I don't always succeed, but I do try.

My wife of over 30 years and I own a small farm where I raise milk goats, rabbits, chickens and a garden. I raise—depending on the weather and bugs—between forty and sixty percent of our food mostly organically. By "mostly" I mean if it looks like I will lose an animal I will do what I think is necessary. We make no trash; we use or recycle everything.

I lived for fourteen years of my life without electricity or running water. I had my only son naturally with no drugs. Though I was married off at sixteen (in an attempt to keep me from being gay) to a thirty-four-year-old man who immediately took me to New York and stuck me in a drug den for a month, I have smoked a total of five joints in my life. I have never done any other drugs. My son was a prescription drug addict for nine years.

I have worked every shit job you can imagine from pulling car parts in a junk yard and cleaning rich people's houses to home health care. I ran an industrial plane and have logged timber using a team of mules. I have worked at saw mills, framed houses, and poured slabs. I am a carpenter and a rock mason. I can run (install) electricity, and I can plumb (I hate plumbing). I have also built more than one house using only hand tools and a chain saw. I like to hike and cave, and I love the ocean.

I fought heavy weapons (and trained other fighters) with the SCA for about twelve years. During that time I broke several bones, and I have a seven-inch plate and eight screws in my left arm as a result of a bastard sword blow. Elizabeth Moon talked me into fencing many years ago and I still do that, but I sold all my armor and heavy weapons last year. Erin Grey talked me into trying Tai Chi to help with my CFS, so I have now been doing do a mixture of Tai Chi and Chi Gung every day for the last five years.

Mercedes Lackey helped me get my first short story sale in Marion Zimmer Bradley's magazine. That sale opened the door for others to MZB, one of which was included in a German-language anthology, and the royalties came in steadily for many years.

CJ Cherryh line edited the first two chapters of Chains of Freedom and taught me more about writing doing that than I had learned to that point.

I'm not just name-dropping here; I'm giving credit to people who helped me who certainly didn't have to. Over the years I've come to know many very famous people, and here's what I know for sure—we are ALL the same.

In the writing community the person who is the most famous and makes the most money is often the least talented or deserving—not always, but often. In our business who makes it and who doesn't is often determined by nothing in the world but dumb-ass luck. That being the case, the near worship we see of the "famous" is something I just don't get at all.

The truth is I always think bios are sort of a waste. Anyone who reads my work knows more about the real me than I could ever put in a bio. If you want to talk to me, find me on Facebook. If you see me somewhere, come right up and talk to me. I am just like you. Luckily, I have a job I love, and the reason I have this great job is that people like you let me.

About the Cover Artist

Sherri Dean lives in a small town outside Kansas City, Missouri. A veteran in the field of Animal Health, she spends her quality time enjoying art, writing, costuming and reading comics.

Her artwork is featured in *Bubbas of the Apocalypse: the Card Game*, and she did the cover for *Recycled*, both available from Yard Dog Press. She enjoys feedback, and her latest works—including her book covers, cards, and t-shirt design—can be seen at the Yard Dog Press site at:
www.yarddogpress.com

Since the first edition of this book, Sherri has become a published author as well. In addition to short stories, Sherri co-authored (with Selina Rosen) the Yard Dog Press title, *Weirdough, Inc.* Check it out on the YDP website or at Amazon.

Yard Dog Press Titles as Of This Print Date

Tales from Keltora, Laura J. Underwood
Tales of the Lucky Nickel Saloon, Second Ave., Laramie, Wyoming, U S of A, Ken Rand
Tarbox Station, Rhonda Eudaly
The Territories (#5 in the Sword Masters Series),, Selina Rosen
Texistani: Indo-Pak Food from a Texas Kitchen, Beverly A. Hale
That's All Folks, J. F. Gonzalez
Through Wyoming Eyes, Ken Rand
Tranquility, Tracy Morris
Turn Left to Tomorrow, Robin Wayne Bailey
The Twins (#4 in the Sword Masters Series),, Selina Rosen
The Undead At My Head, Ethan Nahté
Villains in Training, Julia S. Mandala and Linda L. Donahue
Wandering Lark, Laura J. Underwood
Weirdough, Inc., Selina Rosen and Sherri Dean
Wings of Morning, Katharine Eliska Kimbriel
Zombies in Oz and Other Undead Musings, Robin Wayne Bailey

Fantasy Writers Asylum (A YDP Imprint):

Blood Songs, Julia Mandala
Chaos Heir: Beholden A. D. Guzman
Death's Paladin Christopher Donahue
Gateway to Corimar, Julia Mandala & Linda L. Donahue
Spirit Poles, Julia Mandala & Linda L. Donahue
Tale of the Black Heart, Linda L. Donahue
Traitor's Gate, Linda L. Donahue & Julia Mandala

Double Dog (A YDP Imprint):

#1:
Of Stars & Shadows, Mark W. Tiedemann
This Instance of Me, Jeffrey Turner

#3:
Home Is the Hunter, James K. Burk
Farstep Station, Lazette Gifford

#4:
Sabre Dance, Melanie Fletcher
The Lunari Mask, Laura J. Underwood

#5:
House of Doors, Julia Mandala
Jaguar Moon, Linda A. Donahue

Just Cause (A YDP Imprint):

www.ingramcontent.com/pod-product-compliance
Lightning Source LLC
Chambersburg PA
CBHW030523130626
46549CB00007B/3084